Seeing the Elephant

A STORY OF THE CIVIL WAR

PAT HUGHES   Pictures by KEN STARK

Farrar, Straus and Giroux · New York

The author and illustrator gratefully acknowledge Dr. John David Smith, Charles H. Stone
Distinguished Professor of American History, The University of North Carolina at Charlotte, for his
critical review of the text and art.

Text copyright © 2007 by Pat Hughes
Illustrations copyright © 2007 by Ken Stark
Distributed in Canada by Douglas & McIntyre Ltd.
Color separations by Chroma Graphics PTE Ltd.
Printed and bound in China by South China Printing Co. Ltd.
Designed by Barbara Grzeslo
First edition, 2007
10 9 8 7 6 5 4 3 2 1

www.fsgkidsbooks.com

Library of Congress Cataloging-in-Publication Data
Hughes, Pat (Patrice Raccio).
    Seeing the elephant : a story of the Civil War / Pat Hughes ; pictures by Ken Stark.— 1st ed.
        p.   cm.
    Summary: Ten-year-old Izzie wants to join the war like his older brothers and go into battle against the
Confederate Army, but when he meets a Rebel soldier in a hospital, he begins to see things differently.
    ISBN-13: 978-0-374-38024-3
    ISBN-10: 0-374-38024-4
    1. United States—History—Civil War, 1860–1865—Juvenile fiction. [1. United States—History—Civil War,
1860–1865—Fiction. 2. Soldiers—Fiction. 3. Brothers—Fiction. 4. Toleration—Fiction.] I. Stark, Ken, ill.
II. Title.

PZ7.H87374See 2007
[Fic]—dc22

                                                                        2005052753

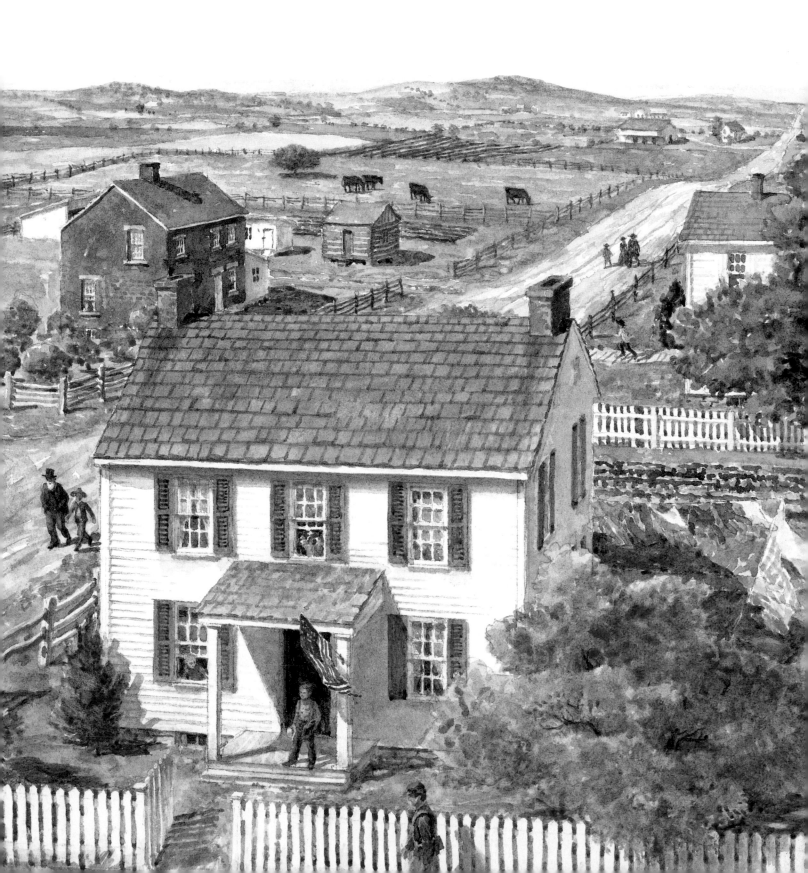

The day my brothers went to war, I waited on the porch so I could be the first to say goodbye.

Ario's the oldest. He came out serious and slow, knelt down, and looked all over my face. "You be a good boy, Iz." Blue woolen coat sleeves scratched my cheek as he smothered me in a hot hug. I was nearly ten, too old for hugging. But just this once, I didn't mind.

Indoors, Calvin clattered down the stairs. He bounded out and rubbed my hair into a tangle. "So long, Iz. I'm off to see the elephant. Come on, Ario! We'll be late."

Cal had told me that "seeing the elephant" was soldier talk for going into battle for the first time. The way he was shifting from foot to foot and yanking on Ario's sleeve, you'd have thought that elephant was waiting right down the road.

"I'll be back soon as I can," Ario told me.

"Yeah, soon as we teach those Rebels to behave," Calvin said with a grin. "Come *on*, Ario. Look for us in the parade, Iz!" he called over his shoulder.

The whole town turned out for the parade. The band played "Yankee Doodle." The new soldiers marched by to cheers and huzzahs.

Ma and Pa and I joined the crowd with my little brothers and sisters—Annie, Bartie, Frank, and baby Bessie.

Pa held the baby high, and everybody waved hands and hats and Stars and Stripes. But Ma didn't wave as my brothers passed by. She had turned her face, pressing a handkerchief to her eyes.

I didn't think it was fair that Ario and Cal got to fight the Rebels while I had to stay way up here in Pennsylvania with all these children. I wanted to see the elephant, too, and teach the Rebels to behave.

But all I saw that summer was the chickens and cows and apple trees at my grandfather's farm. And it turned out that all Ario and Cal saw was soldiers marching along dusty roads.

I wrote to them both, but I got only one reply:

Dear Izzie,

So far no battles, but plenty of drilling and marching. The food is not too bad!

How is the farm this year? I would like to be home by Thanksgiving, but it doesn't look as if that will happen. The Rebels have done a terrible thing, splitting up our country this way. And it's up to us soldiers to make them stop it.

Write again. Kiss the babies for me. I know you love that sort of thing!

Affectionately,
Ario

In the fall, Pa and Ma told us Calvin was in a hospital. He had typhoid, a bad disease that gives you fever and headaches and muscle aches. But Calvin was resting now, and they said he would be all right.

"Will he come home?" I asked.

"No," Pa said. "He wants to rejoin the regiment as soon as he's able."

That made me proud. Calvin was tough. He'd stay and fight till the Rebels were whipped.

"Won't the war be over soon, Pa?" Annie asked.

"We thought so back in April, darling. But now . . ." Pa didn't finish the sentence.

Finally, a letter came from Cal.

> Dear Iz,
>
> I am a lot better now, and back with my company. If you ever go to war, don't go with Ario. He is always telling me what to do and when to rest. He wants me to ride a horse when the other men are marching. I won't do it. I feel ashamed. The marching does tire me, though. Don't tell Pa and Ma. They thought I should muster out after the typhoid, but I want to see that elephant.
>
> Write again and tell me all the news.
>
> Cal

Christmas wasn't the same without my brothers. I missed them so much, I lay down before the fire and wrote to them together.

Dear Ario and Cal,

It is Christmas night. We had our goose with Grandma and Grandpa. Frank was so naughty when they arrived. Grandma spoke to him and he called her a nasty pig! Pa was terribly embarrassed. Then everyone turned to me and asked where Frank had learned such a thing.

My favorite presents were new ice skates and the book *Robinson Crusoe*. Annie got a doll and Bartie got a locomotive that you wind up. Frank ate too much and threw up. One candle came near to setting the tree on fire.

I wish you could come home. Then we would go skating, Cal. And Ario, you would read to us afterward. Tell me about your Christmas.

From
Izzie

Ario wrote back. He said that Cal would not take it easy and that the soldiers got nothing for Christmas dinner but soft bread and some barley. It made me sad and mad. I wished they'd hurry up and beat those Rebels and end this war.

One afternoon, I arrived home to the terrible sound of Ma crying. Cal! I thought. He's dead! Heart pounding, I crept to the parlor door. Pa was there with Ma, and I heard anger, not sorrow, in his voice. "He seems determined to throw his life away! The foolish boy, he—"

Then they spotted me.

"Oh, Izzie," Ma sighed.

I was much too old for crying, but I ran into her arms.

"It's all right, Iz," Pa said, waving a letter. "Calvin's had another bout with typhoid, but it appears the worst is behind him. He's in Philadelphia. I must go and bring him home."

Each day for a week, I raced back from school. Each day, Ma met me at the door with a sad smile. "Not yet, Iz."

Finally, on Saturday morning, Annie and Bartie and I were playing marbles on the parlor floor when Ma sang out, "They're here!" I tried to rush outside, but she clapped a hand on my shoulder. I followed her solemn stare to the sidewalk, where Pa was helping Calvin from the carriage.

Cal looked lost in his civilian clothes. He hobbled with a cane, eyes fixed on the ground, face pale and pained. Pa tried to take his arm, but Calvin scowled him off. Up the walk they came with a terrible slowness. I wished my aunt Bell were here. She was a nurse, and she'd have been able to help. But she was in the war, too, in Washington, D.C.

Cal struggled to climb the porch stairs and stopped in front of Ma.

She hugged him. "Oh, Cal" was all she said, and then he shrugged away.

He paid no attention to the rest of us, just walked right past.

Ma told me not to worry, Cal would soon be back to his old self.
But he kept to his bed even after the doctor said he was well enough to
get up, and I wrote to Ario for advice. The day I got his reply, I went up
to see Calvin after dinner. He had hardly eaten anything, just rearranged
the food on his plate. "Didn't you like the roast?" I asked.

"I wasn't all that hungry."

"Oh." I sat on his bed. "I have a letter from Ario. He still hasn't seen
the elephant. He says he doesn't think there *is* any elephant!" I said, and
I heard that my laugh sounded fake.

"Right," Calvin answered sarcastically.

"I brought the checkers up," I said. "Do you want to play?"

"No, *Israel*, I don't."

It badly hurt my feelings, him saying my real name in such a scornful way. But Ario had written that it would take Cal a while to feel better about missing the war. Be kind, he'd said. So I tried again.

"Cal . . . I'm sorry you had to muster out. I know you wanted to whip the Rebels. But I think—"

"I need no lecture from a ten-year-old!" he interrupted fiercely. "All right, Iz? And get off my bed! Just let me be, would you?"

I ran out of the room—and there was Pa, standing in the hall like a grim statue. He marched into Cal's room and slammed the door, but I heard every word.

"I've had enough of your surly behavior and moping around! The war is over for you, Calvin, and you'd best accept that like a man! It is time for you to get out of that bed! And I expect you to treat this family with the same kindness and respect we have been showing you. Do I make myself clear?"

I barely heard Cal answer, "Yes, Pa."

"Good!"

As Pa's footsteps neared the door, I scurried down the stairs.

Walking home from school the next day, I realized spring had truly returned. Daffodils and dogwoods bloomed, robins hopped, and it was so warm I carried my coat. As I reached our porch, I saw Calvin sitting in the sun. I tried to sneak past, but he called, "Hey, Iz."

I stopped.

"You want to get the checkers?" he asked, and we both smiled.

When Aunt Bell had leave, she came to visit us. I could see at dinner that Cal was uneasy with talk of the battles and the wounded. If a soldier had to muster out, he'd told me, he ought to have a gunshot to show for himself, instead of some blasted fever.

After dessert, Aunt Bell turned to me. "Izzie," she said, "if your parents agree, I'll take you back to Washington for a while."

Before I had a moment to get excited, Ma said, "Oh, Bell, no . . ."

"It's perfectly safe," Aunt Bell told her, and then she looked at Pa. "You know I'd never suggest it otherwise."

"What do you think, dear?" Ma asked Pa.

"Please?" I said in a small voice.

Pa studied me as if he'd find the answer on my face.

Then Calvin said, "You know what I think?" Nobody had asked his opinion, but he gave it just the same. "I think you should let him go."

Aunt Bell and I took one train to Philadelphia, then another to Washington. All along the way, there were soldiers. Soldiers with haversacks, soldiers with weapons, soldiers with canteens.

Soldiers writing letters and cracking jokes. Everywhere I looked,
I saw blue. The ride was slow and horribly hot.

By the time we reached Washington, I felt sick to my stomach and very sleepy. Aunt Bell's boardinghouse was near a building that had been turned into a hospital. She put me to bed on her trundle, and I fell asleep listening to omnibus horses clomping past the window.

Every day, Aunt Bell went to the wards. And every day, she left me in the care of her landlady, Mrs. Waring, who had a girl of three and a tiny baby. I didn't like this arrangement at all.

"Why can't I go out and walk around on my own?" I asked Aunt Bell one morning.

"You don't know the town yet, Iz. What if you got lost?"

"Then why can't I go with you?"

"The hospital is no place for a little boy, Iz."

"I'm not little!"

"I think it would disturb you to see the wounded men, dear."

"Well, what was the use in coming?" I complained. "If I wanted to sit around all day and play with babies, I'd have stayed home!"

"Iz, don't vex me, please. Tonight is the President's levee. Would you like to go?"

Go to the White House and meet Mr. Lincoln? "Yes!" I nearly shouted.

"Then behave yourself. If I have a bad report, you shall not go."

The reception was crowded with all kinds of people standing in a line that crept along like a lazy snake. I was too excited to be impatient, though we waited forever. Finally, we saw President Lincoln. I fixed my eyes on him as we moved closer and closer. He smiled at everyone, nodding and shaking hands.

"He looks tired," Aunt Bell whispered to me. "And terribly sad."

"But he's smiling."

"Yes," she said with a sigh.

When we reached the President, I was so scared I couldn't open my mouth. He said hello to Aunt Bell, and as she shook his hand she said, "Oh, Mr. Lincoln, it must be trying, to greet so many."

"I am rewarded by seeing all the lovely ladies," he replied, and then he looked at me. "What is your name, young man?"

"Izzie." My throat felt stuffed with cotton.

"Israel," Aunt Bell corrected.

"And how old are you, Israel?"

"Ten," I squeaked.

"You're nearly grown! Are you a good boy, Izzie?"

I opened my mouth to answer, but Aunt Bell got there first. "Sometimes," she said, and the President threw his head back and laughed.

Then we had to move along.

"What'd you tell him *that* for?" I asked angrily.

"Well," she said with a little smile, "I think when the President of the United States asks a question, he ought to have a truthful answer."

Ario's regiment was nearby, but he wrote that he could not get to Washington to see how much I'd changed. So Aunt Bell had my picture made, and we sent it to him. One day she took me to the museums and to watch the building of the Capitol, and we walked along the Potomac River.

That night, a knock on our door woke me up. Aunt Bell rushed into the hall, and I heard her whispering with Mrs. Waring.

When Aunt Bell came back, she lit a candle.

"What is it?" I asked, sitting up.

"There's been a battle. The wounded are arriving by train. I must go."

"Did we beat the Rebels?"

"Oh, Iz, I don't know." Aunt Bell sounded impatient and a little angry. "Now hide your face while I dress."

As I sat with my eyes covered, I thought of something that made my heart thump hard. "Aunt Bell? Do you think Ario was in it?"

"I'm not sure, dear."

"Can't I come along?"

"Of course not," she said sharply. "You'd be in the way." I didn't answer, and she said in a softer voice, "Listen, Iz. I'll send word the moment I find out about Ario's regiment. Tomorrow I'll take you to visit the soldiers." She kissed my forehead and pinched out the candle. "Good night."

"Aunt Bell?" I said. "If you see Ario . . ." But I couldn't finish the sentence.

I couldn't fall back to sleep, either, so that whole long next day I was tired—tired and bored. I wanted to see a piece of this war, and I wished Aunt Bell would hurry back and take me to it. But she didn't come, and she didn't send word. All day, people stopped in to talk. We heard many had been killed and wounded in the terrible battle. And it was still going on.

Aunt Bell returned late, so weary she could hardly walk. But she managed these words as she sank into a soft parlor chair: "Ario was in the battle, but he was not hurt."

In the morning, Aunt Bell took me to the hospital. She was right. What I saw there *did* upset me. I stayed close as she moved from soldier to soldier, dressing their wounds, bathing their fevered faces.

Finally, she spoke to me. "Come, Iz. There's someone who wants to meet you. I told him about you yesterday."

I trailed behind her till we reached a pale soldier whose right arm was missing. Aunt Bell laid a hand on his shoulder. "Say hello to Private Kyle, Izzie. Grafflin, this is that nephew of mine."

"I'm mighty pleased to meet you, young feller," he said, and by his talk I could tell he was a Southerner.

I just could not believe it! First Aunt Bell went and told President Lincoln I was good only sometimes. And now she expected me to visit with a Rebel!

"I've got a brother your size back home," he told me.

"I've got a brother *your* size," I fired back, "and he's out shooting you Rebs!"

"Israel!" Aunt Bell gasped, but the Rebel laughed softly.

"That's all right, Miss Bell. I reckon my brother'd be about as mouthy to any Yankee he'd come across."

"Nurse!" somebody called. "Will you help me with this patient?"

Aunt Bell scurried off, leaving me with the Rebel. I stared at him hard. I felt a little sorry because of his arm, but what did he expect? When you took up weapons against your own country, you had to accept what came.

"What's your brother's regiment?" he asked me. He had straw-colored hair, and his eyes seemed very blue.

"Ario's with the Twenty-eighth Pennsylvania."

"Is that where you're from? Pennsylvania?"

"Yes," I said. I knew Mama would want me to be polite, since he was so badly hurt. So I asked, "Where are you from?"

"South Carolina."

"South Carolina!" That got me mad all over again. "You're the ones who *started* this war!"

He chuckled in that quiet way. "Oh, we did, did we?"

"You sure did! You fired on Fort Sumter!"

"Hmmm . . . Well, there's truth to that, Izzie. But I think of it like this. What if you were playing with some friends in your yard back home? And you had a fight with those friends and told 'em to get out of your yard, you didn't want to play with 'em anymore. And they didn't go. What would you do?"

"In my own yard? I'd run 'em out, that's what!"

"There you go." He grinned. "Fort Sumter. You Yankees wouldn't get out of our yard!"

I'd never thought of it that way, and at first, I didn't know how to answer. Then I remembered what my brothers had told me. "You Rebels split up our country. You had no right to do that."

"Well now, *I* didn't split up the country, Izzie. I reckon it's the politicians, North and South, who have got to take the blame for that. But my home was invaded, and I had to come to her defense. If that's a crime"—he raised his only hand—"I'm guilty."

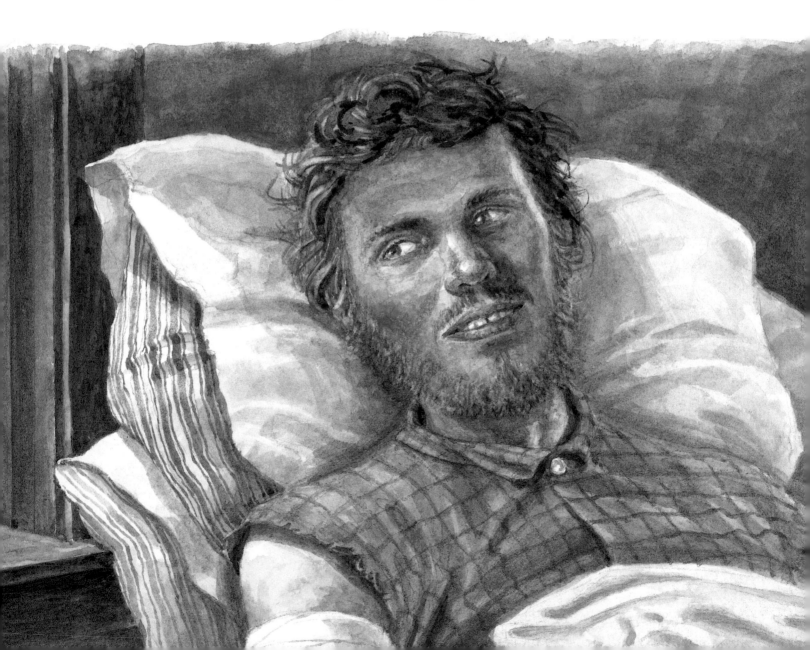

Once more, I was stuck for a reply. So I said, "What kind of a dumb name is Grafflin, anyway?"

He laughed hard. "Well, what kind of a dumb name is Ario?" he asked, and then I had to laugh with him.

"It's Ariovistus," I said. "And it's my papa's name, too. And his papa before him."

"Well, *that's* a coincidence. Same with me and my pappy and my grandpappy! They call me Graff at home. Here, Izzie. Would you like to see a picture of my little brother?"

"Mmm . . . I suppose it couldn't hurt."

Graff slid the photograph out from right under the blanket. "That's us both. We had it made before I left."

"What's his name?" I asked.

"Travis."

I kept staring at the picture. "You have any other brothers or sisters?"

"Three sisters, in between Travis and me. How about you, Izzie?"

"I've got a bunch, mostly younger. But between Ario and me, there's Calvin. He was in the war, too, but he got typhoid twice and had to muster out."

"Well, he's the lucky one."

"He sure doesn't see it that way. He wanted to stay and make you Rebels behave."

"Make a Rebel behave! Now, there's a tall order!"

For somebody with one arm just gone, Graff sure did laugh a lot. But he was starting to seem weary, and this time his grin faded to a grimace.

"Your wound hurting you?" I asked.

"Naw . . . not too bad."

"I guess you'll be going home now, right?"

"Izzie." He pressed his hand flat to his chest. "I'm captured. From here, I go to prison."

My face burned with embarrassment. "I forgot," I mumbled.

"Never mind," he said. "Anyhow, I'd like to write to Travis before I leave here. Tell him what's happened. But I lost my writing hand."

"You want me to write for you?" I said quickly.

"I would be much obliged."

Aunt Bell came back. "Tell me, Grafflin, how many times has he insulted you?"

"Just once, ma'am," he said, nodding thoughtfully.

"I didn't!" I protested.

"My dumb name?" he reminded me in his quiet voice.

"Oh, that," I said, and we both laughed. "Aunt Bell, can I write a letter for him?"

Aunt Bell laid her hand on Graff's cheek. "Tomorrow, perhaps. I think Grafflin needs to get some rest."

Graff nodded, closing his eyes for a second. "Will you come tomorrow, Izzie?"

"I sure will."

All evening, I couldn't stop talking about Grafflin. I told Aunt Bell what he'd said about the war and how it had made me think.

"Perhaps I shouldn't have introduced you," Aunt Bell said. "It's an awful lot for a little boy."

"I'm *not little*! And besides, I like him, Aunt Bell. You *will* let me see him again, won't you?"

"I suppose." She sighed. "Back home, it all seems very clear. But things aren't quite so simple here, are they, Iz?"

"No," I replied. "They're not."

Aunt Bell did let me see Graff in the morning, but not until she had changed his bandages. Then she got me a box to lean on to write his letter.

"How do you feel?" I asked him.

"Oh, not so bad, Iz." But he looked worse than yesterday, and he sounded more tired.

I knelt on the floor, laying out the paper on the box. I uncapped the ink and dipped my pen. "Ready."

"Dear Travis," Graff said. "Right off, I will explain why this letter doesn't look to be coming from me. I am in a Washington hospital, captured wounded, my right arm shot off. I met a boy who is writing for me. He is a Yankee, but don't get mad. He has been awful kind to me. His aunt is my nurse, and she is an angel." Graff shut his eyes, took a breath, and continued. "I suppose you're wondering if you'll have to do all the plowing from now on."

"Plowing?" I couldn't help but interrupt.

When Graff opened his eyes, there was a twinkle in them. "Izzie, don't you know what plowing is?"

"Sure I do. But why do *you* have to do any?"

"Because I live on a farm!"

"Don't your slaves do that sort of thing?"

Graff burst out with a laugh that turned me red.

"Oh, I'm sorry, Iz," Graff said. "Truly I am. We have no slaves. Just a few acres and some hogs, and two scrofulous boys to work beside their pappy."

"I didn't know," I mumbled.

"Course you didn't, Iz," he said. "Course not."

"All right," I said a little gruffly. "Go on."

"Let's see . . . all the plowing from now on. If that's so, I'll find ways to make it up to you. Travis, listen here. I will be sent to prison after this. Promise you'll be a good, brave boy no matter what. Obey Mama and Pappy. Be a good brother to our sisters, and kiss them for me. And when you kneel beside our bed at night, remember me to God, and pray I make it home."

It was all I could do to keep my tears from splashing onto the page. Then he finished quietly, "Your loving brother, Graff."

His eyes were closed again, and he was wearing a peaceful smile. But now his face was all sweaty, and when he swallowed, his Adam's apple bobbed up and down hard and he made a pained face.

"Graff? You all right?"

"Thanks, Iz," he said. "I feel much . . . better . . . now."

Then Aunt Bell was at my side. "He needs to rest, Iz," she said lightly, but I saw worry in her face as she wiped Graff's forehead with a wet cloth. "Come. Let's send that letter on its way."

Next day when I awoke, Aunt Bell was already dressed and sitting in a chair by the window. I jumped up to put on my clothes. "Can we go to the hospital?" I asked. "I want to see how Graff is."

"Iz, I've been at the hospital most of the night," she said slowly. "Didn't you hear me leave?"

"No. Was there another battle?"

"No."

"Good. Can we go and see Graff now?"

"Izzie . . . Graff's gone."

"What!" I protested. "They took him to prison already? He's too sick! Why'd they have to—"

"Iz," Aunt Bell interrupted. "Not to prison. He's gone to God."

I couldn't breathe, or move, or say a word.

"Gangrene had set in to the wound," Aunt Bell explained. "Nothing could be done. He asked for me, and I was with him at the end. He wanted you to have this."

She held out the picture of Graff and his brother.

At that I burst out crying and hugged Aunt Bell, not caring *how* old I was. She cried, too, and blamed herself for my sorrow. But I was glad I'd gotten to know Graff and to hear his side. I knew I'd never forget my Rebel.

Later, Aunt Bell let me go out by myself. As I walked along the Potomac, I decided to write to Ario and tell him to be very careful. Then I'd write to Travis about how sorry I was. But first, I had something to say to Cal:

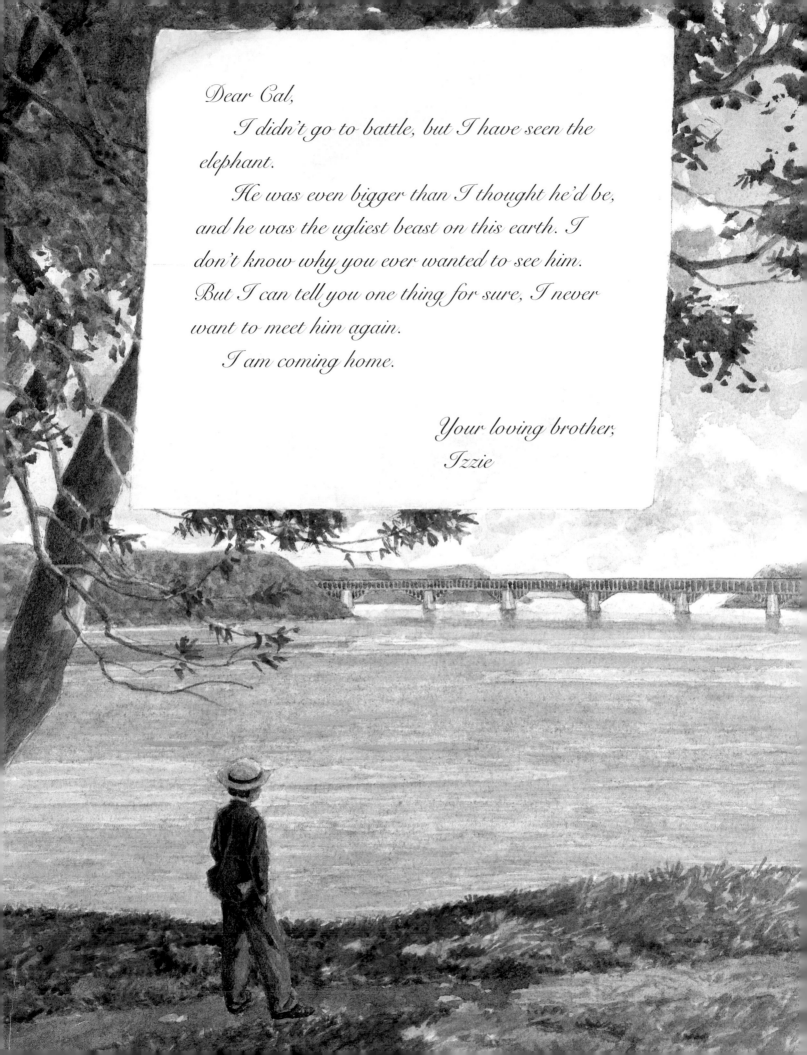

Dear Cal,

    I didn't go to battle, but I have seen the elephant.

    He was even bigger than I thought he'd be, and he was the ugliest beast on this earth. I don't know why you ever wanted to see him. But I can tell you one thing for sure, I never want to meet him again.

    I am coming home.

                      Your loving brother,
                      Izzie

Izzie Pardee

Author's Note

During the Civil War, young Israel Pardee—great-grandfather of my husband, Samuel Hughes—left Hazleton, Pennsylvania, to spend time in Washington, D.C., with his aunt Bell Robison, who was an Army nurse there. Bell wrote a number of letters about their experiences. Izzie's meeting with President Lincoln and the making of Izzie's photograph really did happen pretty much as I have written.

But it was this mysterious line in one of Bell's letters that inspired my story: "I think Izzie will be ready to come home soon, as he has seen the elephant." I knew what it meant to see the elephant, but how did it apply to this ten-year-old? Although the Pardees were a staunch Union family, I like to think that when confronted with human suffering, the real Izzie would have reacted just as the imagined Izzie did.

Many more details in the story are factual. Izzie's brothers were both with the Twenty-eighth Pennsylvania Volunteer Infantry in the early stages of the war. Young Calvin Pardee did muster out after two bouts with typhoid; Ario Pardee, Jr., went on to command the 147th PVI and saw the elephant at Antietam, Chancellorsville, Gettysburg, Peach Tree Creek, and numerous other battles and skirmishes. At Gettysburg National Military Park, a monument on Pardee Field commemorates the bravery of Ario and his 147th Regiment.

The Civil War correspondence of the Pardee and Robison families— fictionalized here—was privately published as *Dear Pa . . . And So It Goes* (1971) by Gertrude Keller Johnston. I would like to express my sincere affection for this lady, whom I never knew. I am so grateful that she appreciated the value of the past.